A LEEG
OF HIS OWN

Croaking Bullfrogs,
Hidden Robbers

NOX PRESS

books for that extra kick to give you more power

www.NoxPress.com

A LEEG
OF HIS OWN

Croaking Bullfrogs,
Hidden Robbers

Elise Leonard

NOX PRESS
books for that extra kick to give you more power

www.NoxPress.com

Leonard, Elise
A Leeg of His Own series / Croaking Bullfrogs, Hidden Robbers
ISBN 978-1-935366-08-9

Printed in the U.S.A.
First Nox Press printing: March 2009

NOX PRESS

books for that extra kick to give you more power

Hey,

*I hear the **Bronx** is in the house!*

This book is dedicated to Mr. Deven Black
and his cool students at MS 127 in the Bronx.

Lou Holtz is quoted to have said,
"Ability is what you are capable of doing.
Motivation determines what you do.
Attitude determines how well you do it."
(If you don't know who Lou Holtz is, look him up.
He's an amazing man!)

To Mr. Black:
thank you for showing your students what they are
capable of doing.

To Mr. Black and his students:
thank you for finding the motivation to do what you do.

To Mr. Black's students:
keep up the great attitude!
(Hey, James! Yeah, I heard about you.)

To Mr. Black and all of the many other dedicated,
concerned, caring, *true* educators:
we need more like you!

Special thanks to Mark and the folks at
Party City in Tampa, FL
for helping us get the cover photo!

~Elise

CHAPTER 1

I was using my once-a-month bathroom pass.

We were only allowed to leave class once a month. And this was my day.

On my way to the bathroom, I heard chanting. It was in the distance, but it was definitely there.

"Free the frogs!"

"Free the frogs!"

"Free the frogs!"

Since I was only allowed out once a month? I figured I might as well live it up a little.

So I walked toward the chanting. You know, just to check it out.

"Free the frogs!"

"Free the frogs!"

As the chanting got louder? I knew I was in the right place.

I peeked into Mr. Vassu's classroom. (That's where all the noise was coming from.)

I didn't know what I'd expected to see.

But it wasn't Annie.

And I *sure* didn't expect to see her standing on top of

Mr. Vassu's desk.

She was leading the chant.

I was shocked.

So I was standing there. Outside of Mr. Vassu's class. Just staring at Annie. On top of Mr. Vassu's desk. Chanting like a maniac. Getting everyone all riled up.

In a way, she was kind of, well, inciting a riot.

Then, out of nowhere, Abbie came flying down the hallway.

"Annie *needs* me," Abbie cried as she crashed right into me.

Before I could get up, she blew right past me. She tore open Mr. Vassu's door. And out came flopping a whole army of joyful frogs.

They were hopping everywhere!

Big green, ugly, croaking Mexican jumping beans. Just flailing every which way.

It was total chaos!

I was just getting up when I saw the principal.

Mrs. Caldor was bustling down the frog-infested hallway.

Let's just say, she wasn't too happy.

"What are you people up to now?!" she barked.

She tsked a few times for good measure.

"They're always up to something!" she muttered to herself.

I took offense.

"I was just going to the bathroom," I said honestly.

"Right!" she sputtered.

"*Really*," I protested.

She eyed me with disbelief. "So you had *nothing* to do with trashing the science lab?"

"Well, yeah," I said.

"*I think not!*" she snapped. "Now wait here!"

It wasn't a long wait.

First she burst into the science lab. Then she demanded that Annie get off the teacher's desk. After that? It was a blur.

All I knew was that when the dust finally settled? Annie, Abbie and I were in her office.

Sitting in the principal's waiting room. Waiting to get picked up.

"What just happened here?" I asked.

"You don't know?" Annie asked me.

I shook my head.

I looked at Annie.

"I was going to the bathroom. Then I heard chanting," I said.

I looked at Abbie.

"Then *you* knocked me over," I added.

Then I looked between the two of them.

"And now we're all here," I finished.

Annie looked embarrassed.

Abbie didn't.

"I'm sorry, Andrew," Annie said. "This is all my fault."

"No it's not," Abbie cut in.

"It's not?" Annie asked Abbie. "How is this not my fault?"

"If the *school* didn't make us do such barbaric things, *you* wouldn't have gotten into trouble."

"I just couldn't let them all die," Annie squeaked.

Abbie nodded.

"And then be cut open," Annie added softly.

"In this day and age? With computer simulations? It's *barbaric*!" Abbie voiced loudly.

The bell rang.

My friends Raul and Snoop slipped into the principal's waiting room.

"What's up?" Snoop asked.

He looked from me to Annie to Abbie.

I shrugged.

Raul looked at Annie. "Is it true? You incited a riot?"

Annie turned beet red. "Only a little one," she whispered.

"And you let all the frogs loose?" Snoop asked her.

Annie looked at Snoop. "I couldn't let them die for no reason."

Snoop nodded at Annie.

Then he looked at me. He nodded his chin my way. "And what's *your* part in all this?"

I stared at him blankly. "I have no clue."

"So what now?" Raul asked.

Snoop knew the drill. "In-school suspension?"

Abbie rolled her eyes. "Get this! Thanks to the flu outbreak?"

"There are no extra teachers around," Annie continued.

"So there *is* no in-school suspension," I finished.

"So you're off the hook?" Raul said hopefully.

"Pfft," Abbie scoffed. "Yeah, right."

"They called our parents," I explained.

"We're being sent home," Annie said sadly.

Mr. Vassu opened the door to the principal's waiting room.

He peeked his head in and saw us sitting there. He decided to come in.

Snoop and Raul took that as their cue to leave.

"Good, luck," Raul called over his shoulder.

"See ya. Wouldn't wanna *be* ya," Snoop said as he left the room.

The door closed with a click.

Mr. Vassu walked straight to Annie. He knelt before her.

"Why did you *do* that?" he asked Annie gently.

She told him what she'd told us.

You know. About killing the frogs.

"But you're such a good student, Annie," he countered.

We all looked at her.

She blushed.

He was trying to understand all of this. I could tell.

"You *never* cause any problems," he said to Annie.

Then he looked at Abbie.

I knew what he was thinking. He couldn't say the same about *her*.

Abbie was *always* causing problems.

Me? I was somewhere in between those two in that regard.

Sometimes I got into trouble. Sometimes I didn't.

But Abbie? She was usually right in the middle of trouble. Stirring it up.

Annie? She was rarely in trouble.

Out of the three of us? She was the good one.

CHAPTER 2

"What's *your* problem?!" Abbie snipped at me.

"*You're* my problem!" I snapped back.

"Why don't you shut up!" she said snottily.

"Why don't *you* shut up?" I returned with a nasty sneer.

She threw her hands to her hips. Her face a mask of pure fury.

"Oh. Very mature," she finally said.

"*You're* very mature," I responded quickly.

Okay. So it wasn't my best comeback. But sometimes I just couldn't help it. Sometimes? She made me so mad? I couldn't even *think* straight!

This was obviously one of those times.

Oh, and unless you haven't guessed? I was fighting with my sister.

Abbie.

She could *really* tick me off!

There's just something about her. She really gets under my skin.

And lucky for me? I'm stuck with a carbon copy of her, too.

Yeah, that's right. She's got a twin sister. Annie.

But if you *really* want to get confused? I'll tell you that I'm not just their brother.

I'm sort of their twin, too.

Well, we're triplets.

That's right.

There's *three* of us!

Triplets.

And you want to know something? We've been fighting since, well… probably as far back as the womb!

I don't remember much about those days. But I'm pretty positive we fought even back then. It probably went down something like this:

Me: "Hey. I can't see who's doing it, because it's dark in here. But how about getting your elbow out of my ribs?!"

Annie: "Oh. I'm sorry. It's kind of tight in here." She moved her elbow. "But can you *please* get your cold foot off my back?"

(In case it was me, I probably tried to move my foot.)

Abbie: "I don't even want to *know* whose it is. But whoever has their *butt* in my face? *Move it! NOW*!"

We always seem to get on each others' last nerve.

But that's probably because, as I mentioned, we've never been able to get away from each other.

God. What I wouldn't have done for a single occupancy way back then!

Mostly because it was—and always *is*, and always

will be—two against one.

That's right. They always side together.

And it's always against me.

I don't care how stupid the fight is. It always ends up… two against one. Them against me.

I *never* win.

Ever!

I mean, if I were a *twin*? I'd have a fifty-fifty chance of winning.

But no. I'm a triplet.

So that means someone always loses.

And that loser? It's always *me*!

Of course my parents couldn't have made two *boys* and one *girl*. Right? No.

That might've been pretty *cool*.

Having a *brother* who was always on your side? Letting the "two against one" thing fall in *my* favor a time or two? Or a million?

Yeah, that could've worked out well.

But no.

They had to create two girls… and me!

Thanks a *lot*, Mom and Dad!

So in a nutshell? When the doctor said, "Mr. and Mrs. Leeg? You're having triplets. One boy, and two girls. Congratulations!" my life was pretty much ruined from that moment in time.

Mrs. Franks came out from Mrs. Caldor's office. She

was Mrs. Caldor's assistant.

"I'm sorry, kids. Mrs. Caldor reached your mother at the hospital."

"So she's coming to get us?" Annie asked.

"Just great," I muttered.

"Mom's going to nag us all day long about this," Abbie said.

I looked at Abbie. "All *day*?!" I stammered.

She rolled her eyes. "Yeah, you're right. We'll be hearing about this for *months*."

"Forget any privileges!" Annie said sadly.

"We'll be happy to get bread and water for the next few weeks," I told them.

"Talk about a sentence fitting the crime?!" Abbie grumbled.

Mrs. Franks smiled. "It won't be *that* bad."

The three of us stared at her.

"I know your mother," she said with a little chuckle. "Your mother's a sweetheart."

"Having my mother take off from *work*?" I said.

"To get *us*?" Abbie added.

"For causing *trouble*?" Annie finished.

"This is going to be gruesome," I concluded.

Mrs. Franks laughed. "Well then it's a good thing this flu is going around," she said.

"If the flu wasn't going around, we'd have in-school suspension," Annie corrected her.

"Yeah," I agreed. "And Mom wouldn't have to come

get us at all."

"We'd be out of the woods," Abbie noted.

Mrs. Franks laughed again. "With this flu thing going around, your mom's swamped. The hospital's *filled* with people."

"Oh, man," I said.

"Yes," Annie agreed.

"Now she's *really* going to be ticked off at us," Abbie summed up.

Mrs. Franks laughed again.

I'm so glad our troubles could humor her.

"She can't come to get you," she explained.

"So we can go back to class?" I asked.

She shook her head. "No. Sorry. Mrs. Caldor called your dad. He's coming to get you now."

"Oh," I said. "Great."

"Our *dad's* coming?" Abbie choked out.

"He's going to be delighted about *this*!" Annie finished.

We all groaned together.

Mrs. Franks laughed.

Snoop picked that moment to pop his head back in.

He opened the door slightly.

Then he looked around the room.

He didn't have the door all the way opened.

So he couldn't see Mrs. Franks' desk.

"Where's Caldor?" he whispered.

"In her office," Mrs. Franks whispered back.

17

Snoop got so startled, he banged his head on the door.

Well, it was more like he banged the *door* on his *head*.

It would have been funny. If I hadn't caught sight of my dad's police car. It was rounding the school's driveway.

"Oh no," Snoop said. "Your dad's here."

"Yeah, I know," I said. "He's coming to get us."

Snoop's face said it all. "You guys are in deep…"

Before Snoop could finish that sentence, Mrs. Caldor bustled out of her office.

She was a large, buxom woman. And seemed to bustle everywhere she went.

She didn't ease into a room. Or glide. She bustled.

Everything to her was a big emergency.

A disaster.

I think "upheaval" was her middle name.

Of course her outlook would get my dad all riled up.

After she got to him? It'll take us a bit of time and effort to get him calmed down again.

But don't worry too much. We'd get him calmed down.

Eventually.

I mean, *Annie* was the one who was really in trouble here.

And she was the most levelheaded of the three of us. She was the most sensible. The even-tempered one.

So my dad's conniption fit shouldn't last too long.

Chapter 3

"May I help you, young man?" Mrs. Caldor asked Snoop.

"No, ma'am," he said as he bowed his head.

It was best not to look at her head on. That seemed to set her off.

"I was just saying goodbye to my friends," he said quietly. Like we'd died or something.

That might not be so far off. Depending on how mad my dad was.

"That is very improper," she said as she bustled over. "You will leave at once!"

Snoop just stood there and looked at the three of us.

"I love you guys," he called to us.

Then his eyes flicked to Abbie. He looked nervous. I guess he was worried that she'd heard him.

But not to worry. She barely noticed that he even existed.

Much less heard him slip with words of love.

Snoop was blushing. I think.

It's hard to tell.

He's African American, so the blush kind of gets lost. But I think he *was* blushing.

"Didn't you hear me, young man?! Leave at *once*!" Mrs. Caldor repeated.

Snoop looked at me. Then he looked at Abbie.

His face registered horror.

I knew he was worried about professing his love to Abbie. But like I said. She rarely even noticed him. So he was safe.

I shook my head and waved my hands.

It was my way of trying to tell him "no harm, no foul."

I hoped he got my meaning.

Otherwise, he'd be a basket case the rest of the day.

Snoop slipped out of the principal's waiting room just as my father slipped in.

Oh, man.

He was *not* happy!

He glared at us.

His face was all red and that little vein on his forehead was pulsing.

That was bad. Very, very bad.

"Pleasure to see you again, Mr. Leeg," Mrs. Caldor said.

He nodded silently.

Wow. He didn't return her pleasantry.

That was a very bad sign.

Mrs. Caldor seemed to get the hint.

"I will allow you to take them post-haste," she said quickly.

"I'll sign them out for you," Mrs. Franks added.

Dad turned to Mrs. Franks.

He looked at her and nodded. Again, silently.

Oh, man. This couldn't get any worse.

When he was quiet like that? It meant he was too angry for words.

He was afraid of what he'd say. Didn't want to "break the dam," as he'd put it before.

This was not good.

"We'll just get in the car," Annie said softly.

He was still glaring at us.

We got up from our seats, and left the room.

Our dad was right behind us.

Mrs. Caldor and Mrs. Franks called goodbye. But he didn't even answer *that*.

We were dead meat!

Annie started getting into the back seat.

Abbie was right behind her.

Leaving me to sit up front with my dad.

Great. Just great.

It was always two against one.

Leave *me* to fend for myself up front with Dad. Nice!

"Annie's up front," my father croaked out.

That was all he said.

Annie was almost in the car and had to back out.

She turned to go toward the front seat. Her face was as white as fresh snow. The poor girl was scared out of her wits. I didn't blame her.

I hadn't been too thrilled when I thought *I'd* have to sit up front with him. And *I* hadn't been the one who *started* this whole mess.

So as she and I jockeyed for our seats, we looked at each other.

I felt badly for her. So I kind of smiled.

You know that kind of smile. Not a happy smile. But one that said, "I'm with you in spirit." Even if you were very glad not to be in their shoes.

On the other hand?

I was stuck in the back seat. With Abbie.

That was as bad as having to sit up front with Dad. Even when he *was* in a mood.

In fact, it might be *worse*! At least Dad could be coaxed out of his mood.

Abbie? She was *always* obnoxious.

There was no coaxing Abbie out of that!

She was *born* that way.

We'd gone five blocks toward home. And Dad still hadn't spoken.

Not a word.

But Abbie? She'd already stuck her twig-like finger at me three times. To get me to move over.

I was already almost hugging the far door.

What more did she want from me?!

It was a stupid question. Because I already knew the answer to it.

She wanted me on the *other* side of the door.

That's right.

Outside the car.

If I'd been running along next to it? Like Barney Rubble on the Flintstones? She'd be happy.

Other than that? She was miserable.

And if Abbie was miserable? Then *I* was going to be miserable.

There was no way around it.

Abbie was poking me for the fourth time when Dad spoke.

"What were you *thinking* about, Annie?" he asked her.

She sighed softly. "Daddy, they're living things. Why should they die just so we can see their insides?"

"It's part of science class," he said without really hearing her.

"There are other ways to see the insides of frogs, Daddy," she argued.

"Like computers," Abbie said from the back.

My dad's eyes flashed in the rear-view mirror. "No comments from the peanut gallery," he pronounced.

Abbie sighed loudly. Not with regret or longing or anything. Just a loud obnoxious sigh.

"I'll get to you two in a minute," my father promised.

Great, I thought. *Just great.*

Here he'd almost forgotten we were *in* the car. And bigmouthed Abbie had to let him know we were still there.

Waiting for his wrath.

Just great!

"Are you an idiot?" I whispered to her.

"*You're* the idiot!" she returned.

"*I'm* not the one who just got Dad's attention," I whispered furiously.

"What?! You think he *forgot* about us?" she started to scream.

"Shut *up*!" I warned quietly. I nodded my head toward Dad.

She went ballistic. Totally lost it. "*You* shut up, you idiot!"

My father jammed on the brakes.

If we hadn't had our seatbelts on? We would've been out the front windshield.

"Don't *make* me stop this car!" he snarled.

I wasn't going to be the one to tell him that he'd *already* stopped the car.

We all sat silently.

Like three little angels.

Abbie wasn't the only one losing it.

"You know, guys," he started. "It's bad enough that they keep cutting the budget at work."

He was working his way up to a full head of steam.

"One of these days? I'm going to be out of a job!" he hollered.

He worried about that. A lot.

"Everyone *else*?" he shouted. "They have a second *kid*. Like *normal* people!"

Oh yeah. We knew where *this* was going.

It wasn't the first time we'd heard it.

"But *me?*" he screeched. "*My* second kid had to be *triplets!*"

Yeah. We knew that.

Tell us something we *didn't* know.

"And because you three always seem to get into *trouble*? I have to be *home* all the time!"

Well, in our defense, it wasn't all the time.

And it wasn't always our fault, either. It's just that people noticed us more. For some reason.

"I've got to keep up my *arrest* record!" he wailed.

We knew that too.

CHAPTER 4

"How can I keep up my arrest record when I'm always home with *you* guys?!" he moaned.

This was a common complaint.

"I have the worst arrest record of the whole department," he said loudly.

We'd heard that before, too.

"And you want to know *why*?" he screamed.

Not really.

"Because I have to take you to the doctors. And dentists. And to ski club. And swim team meets. To math club. The library. Track meets. Friend's houses. Debate team meetings. Dances. Bake-offs. Cookie sales. Scout meetings. To the *freaking mall*!" he exploded.

He put the car in gear.

Then he slowly merged back into the stream of traffic.

We were just about hitting town now. (We had to pass through town to get to or from school.)

My dad was still going on about his problems.

Not as strongly, but he was still going on.

He *was* dying down a little. That was good.

Suddenly Annie screamed. "*Dad*! *Watch out*!"

For the second time in three minutes, my dad

slammed on the brakes.

If he hadn't done that? We'd all be dead.

A big, white sedan hurtled through the intersection. It came flying from the right. Out of nowhere.

My father uttered a few choice words. Words my mother would've been shocked to hear.

"*We* have the right of way," he yelled.

He raised his fist at the back end of the car.

"*Our* light was green!" he stated.

So I guess that meant they had sped through a red light.

"They must be going *ninety*!" he added.

I looked at the speed limit sign. It said forty-five.

"Right through town!" he roared.

"Did you see the driver?" Abbie asked him. "He was as white as a ghost!"

"And the passenger," Annie said with horror. "He had an *ax* in his head! There was blood everywhere! And I think I saw his eye hanging down. By a vein or something!"

Annie shuddered with disgust.

"I saw it," I said. "But I didn't believe my eyes."

"You can't imagine the things I see," my dad said tightly.

"Do you think the guy will live?" Annie asked.

"Who knows," my dad answered.

I'd be amazed if the guy lived. That ax was buried pretty deep in his head.

Not to mention… that eye thing.

"Hang on tight, kids," my dad said.

The tires screeched as we turned left.

We raced after the speeding car.

"Let's give them a police escort," my dad said.

He turned on his sirens and lights. Then he floored that baby.

We were almost right behind them. Almost caught up. Then my dad tried to get around them and in front of them.

You know, for the escort.

That way we could get people out of the way. So they could get to the hospital faster.

"It seems like they won't let us pass," Abbie said.

"They're driving totally out of control," Annie added.

"I would too," I said. "If *I* were driving someone with an ax in his head."

At least we were on route to the hospital.

"When we get to the hospital," Dad started.

He took a curve at seventy miles per hour. It was cool!

"You can explain to your mother what happened at school," he finished.

Great.

We get to *see* her.

I was hoping we'd miss her.

That would've given her time to calm down. Maybe not yell so much.

But here we were. Headed straight for the hospital! At

lightening speed.

Great!

But then something really weird happened.

The guys in the sedan blew past the hospital!

"The driver missed it!" Annie shouted with dismay.

Just then, my dad's car radio crackled.

"All units. All units. Bank robbery on Main Street ten minutes ago," said a woman's voice.

Bank robbery?!

"Suspects fled the scene…" she went on.

I looked at my dad.

She crackled on. "Possibly driving a white Chevy Impala."

"Hey," I said. "Isn't that a white Chevy Impala?" I was pointing.

Right at the car we were, ah, escorting.

Abbie scoffed. "You're as sharp as always, Andy-boy."

"Andrew," I corrected.

I know. She just insulted me.

But the nickname bothered me worse. I don't know why.

But I *do* know that's why Abbie always said it.

"Hey," Annie said loudly.

She had to talk loudly. Between the sirens and the screeching tires? You *had* to speak loudly to be heard.

We all looked at Annie.

"Isn't that Barney?" she all but shouted.

She was pointing to the back of the white Chevy Impala.

I squinted my eyes.

"Barney who?" I asked.

"Just Barney!" she said. "Barney the dinosaur!"

I leaned forward in my seat. Looking.

"Yeah," I said. "It *is* Barney the dinosaur!"

"How'd we miss *that*?!" my father uttered.

"He must've been lying down," Annie answered.

"In the back seat," Abbie added.

"The whole time," I finished.

That vein in my dad's head was throbbing. I could see it all the way from the back seat.

"Isn't that… Mrs. Farnsworth?" my dad asked.

We all looked.

"Yup," I said.

"That's Mrs. Farnsworth," Abbie added.

"The bank's secretary," Annie finished.

"You think she's in on it?" I asked.

The radio crackled once more.

"All units. All units. They *have* a hostage. Repeat. They *have* a hostage."

"It's too dangerous," my dad said.

He slowed the car down.

"What are you *doing*, Dad?!" Abbie shouted.

"They're getting away!" Annie added.

"We're *losing* them!" I finished.

"I can't chase bank robbers with my kids in the car!"

my dad insisted.

"But there's no one else around," Abbie argued.

"And Mrs. Farnsworth is a *hostage*," I added.

"We *have* to help her, Dad," Annie finished.

He couldn't argue with that logic.

He sped up again.

"So I guess the passenger doesn't really have an ax in his head," I mentioned.

Abbie looked at me and shook her head.

The car veered sharply to the right.

We hit that curve at about ninety!

Thanks to the motion, Abbie leaned near me.

Then she punched me and pushed off of me as if it were *my* fault.

"They're all wearing masks," my dad said as he sped to get next to them.

We were just about up to the Impala. Almost next to them.

When a car came toward us.

It was a two-lane highway. One way for each direction.

And at the moment? We were in the *wrong* lane!

We almost hit the oncoming car. Head on! Until Dad stomped on the brakes and wove his way back behind the Impala.

"If I could just get next to them!" he said loudly.

Barney was looking out from the back window.

"Or in front of them," my dad added.

He was determined to get these guys. To save Mrs. Farnsworth.

"Is it me?" Abbie asked. "Or is Barney *laughing* at us?"

I leaned forward and a little to the right to see around Dad's head.

"Yup," I said. "He's laughing at us."

Barney was in the back of the Impala. Pointing at us.

And his big, purple head was shaking. It seemed from laughter.

Chapter 5

"I always hated Barney," Abbie said with contempt.

"I loved him," Annie said wistfully.

I didn't hate *or* love Barney. But that song? It made me want to puke!

I mean, really!

I love you,

You love me,

We're a happy family.

Have you *met* my sister Abbie?!

To me? That song was the biggest crock!

Maybe if I'd only been a twin. With Annie. Maybe then the song wouldn't make me want to hurl.

But with Abbie around? I just couldn't buy the song. At all!

"Sorry, kids," my dad said. "I hate to do this. But…"

He got on the car radio.

"Control? This is Alpha nine nine three. I am in pursuit," he bellowed.

The radio cracked. "Alpha nine nine three. Please state your position."

"We are five blocks west of the hospital. Headed southwest," Dad responded.

There was more crackling. "'We?'" the woman asked.

My dad quickly looked at us and took his right hand off the steering wheel.

He motioned with his pointer finger at us. Then he placed it over his lips.

We got the message.

He didn't want anyone to know we were in the car with him.

But how was he going to explain the "we" part of his comment?

"I am in hot pursuit. I am *with* the suspects. Right on their tail," he said. "*We* are headed southwest."

"Oh," the lady said. "I get it now. Okay, Jules. I mean Alpha nine nine three."

"Is there anyone else on this?" he asked the lady.

"No, Alpha nine nine three. Just you."

My dad put down the radio thing.

"Of course," my father muttered to himself.

He placed both hands on the wheel again. And then he started getting *really* aggressive with the Impala.

I didn't know how Annie or Abbie felt. But I was a bit nervous.

Not that I was a wimp or anything. But I *was* in the back seat. And even though I had my seatbelt on? I was being thrown around like crazy.

I felt like a freshly caught fish. Flopping around all over the place.

Plus. If anything happened to us? I was in the back

seat. In a police car.

You know about that. Right?

The inside handles don't work. So the perps can't escape.

So if something *should* happen? Abbie and I can't get out! (Not that I really cared too much about Abbie.)

I was mostly thinking about *me*!

"Where do you think they're headed?" Annie asked my dad.

"Away from me," he said with a weird laugh.

It wasn't evil. Or maniacal.

But it *was* a little, you know, hyped-up and insane sounding.

At least it was to me.

"What's your location Alpha nine nine three?" the woman on the radio asked.

Dad picked up the radio thing. "About five miles south of the hospital."

"We're sending backup," she said.

"Ten four," he said.

"But it'll take a while, Alpha nine nine three," she said.

"Ten four," he repeated.

He put the radio thing back on its hook.

"Why will it take a while?" Annie asked my dad.

"Many reasons," he replied. "Traffic. The single lanes. We're on the other side of town. And we're far

35

from the precinct."

Annie nodded.

I got an idea. A *great* idea. One that might get us out of trouble.

"So maybe it was *good* that we got in trouble at school," I said.

Abbie caught on quickly. "And you had to come get us."

Annie dove right in, too. Normally, she wouldn't. But remember. It was *Annie* who was the most in trouble.

"So *you* got to be the only one on this case," Annie added.

"Just think about your arrest record," Abbie piped in.

"When you get all these guys!" I finished.

My dad didn't look thrilled. But he didn't look angry.

"Maybe it wasn't so bad, after all," he admitted.

Wow.

Our work here was done.

That was easy.

And all it took was one little bank robber police chase.

If we survived this ordeal? I'd have to thank the bank robbers.

You know, for getting our butts out of the frying pan.

I just hoped we weren't headed for the fire.

I said that because the Impala took a sharp left. And so did we.

We took that turn at about ninety. I'd *swear* we were on two wheels.

"They're headed for the highway," my dad shouted.

He pointed to the radio thing.

Annie handed it to him.

"Gert?" he shouted into the thing. "Are you there, Gert?"

Nothing. Just static.

"Gert!" my father shouted into the thing.

Still nothing.

"Where *are* you, Gert?!" he blared.

Some guy came on the radio.

"I'm sorry. Gert's stepped away from her desk for a moment," he said calmly.

"Are you *kidding* me?!" my father shouted.

The man remained calm.

"No," he said. "I think she went to the ladies room."

My dad went ballistic.

"*Now*?" he roared. "She went to the bathroom *now*?!"

The man was silent.

But really. How was he *supposed* to answer that?

If Gert went to the bathroom, she went to the bathroom.

"Oh," the man said. "Here she comes."

"Good," my father barked into the radio thing.

"Oh wait," the young guy said. "She's stopping to get a doughnut."

My dad's forehead vein was pumping like one of those Texan crude oil machines.

"A *doughnut*?!" he screamed.

"It might be a cruller," the guy said timidly.

"Who *is* this?!" my dad barked.

"Oh. I'm sorry. I'm Tim," the man said cheerily. "I'm an intern."

"Well, Tim?" my dad shouted. "Get your newbie butt over to Gert. Tell her to put *down* the doughnut! Then tell her to get *her* butt on the line with the Feds!"

"The F-F-Feds?" Tim choked out.

"That's right, *Tim*," my dad hollered. "I'm pursuing the bank robbers, and they're headed for the highway."

"The h-h-highway?"

My father rolled his eyes and shook his head.

"And in about ten more minutes?" my father shouted. "They'll cross state lines."

"S-S-State lines?" he stuttered.

"That's right, *Tim*," my dad spat out.

We waited for a response.

We'd waited for nothing. Because none came.

My dad went postal. "So if you people sitting in the precinct don't mind? *Could you put down your doughnuts for a few minutes*?!"

CHAPTER 6

My father was super angry.

I was afraid his vein would burst. It was so ugly, I couldn't look at it anymore.

I turned my head.

"Oh," Tim said. "Here comes Gert now. She must have heard you."

Gert's voice came over the airwaves. "Jules? Jules? Is that you?"

"Of *course* it's me, Gert! Who else would you *think* it is?!"

"I'm sorry, Jules. All this excitement. I had to take a little break." She giggled nervously.

"What am I?! Out here alone?" my father muttered to himself.

"Seems so," Abbie said back to Dad.

"Shhhh!" My father shushed her.

I looked at Abbie and smiled widely.

"Shut up!" she hissed at me.

"*You* shut up" I returned.

"Both of you shut up!" my father shouted at us.

"Ex*cuse* me?" Gert said over the radio.

"Oh dammit!" my father muttered. "You two got me

so annoyed, I held down the button!"

"Tell her you were screaming at the perps," I suggested.

He nodded. "Sorry, Gert. I was conversing with the perps."

"You *got* them?" she said excitedly.

"No," he said as he threw me a dirty look in the rearview mirror. "I was shouting back to their car."

"Oh," Gert said shortly. "What are they saying to you?"

My dad looked nervous. He wasn't so good at lying.

"You know. The usual. Obscenities," he said with a shrug.

"That is *so* rude!" Gert said back.

Dad looked at us and made a face. "It's all part of the job, Gert."

Annie gave Dad a thumbs up.

He'd diffused the problem well. But now he had to deal with the *real* problem.

"You need to call the Feds in on this, Gert," he said more calmly.

"Why?" she asked.

"Because they're heading for the state line," Dad explained.

"Oh," Gert said. "That's not good."

"For us? No. For the thieves? Maybe," my dad replied.

"Okay, Jules. I'll call right away."

"Thanks."

"Oh, and one last thing. Has anyone caught up to you yet?" Gert asked.

"Negative," Dad said.

"Then it's a good thing *you're* on them," she said.

"I guess," he agreed hesitantly.

He looked at us. He was *not* happy about bringing us along on this chase.

"But I won't have jurisdiction once we cross that line. So hurry, Gert. Okay?"

"Okay, dearie," she responded.

Funny. Dad went from "Alpha nine nine three"… to "Jules"… to "dearie."

We kept right after them. But they weren't giving up.

They weren't slowing down either.

Once they hit the highway? They were easily clearing one hundred miles per hour.

So were we.

It was pretty cool.

And pretty scary, too.

"Do you do this every day?" I asked my dad.

"No," he said truthfully. "Not every day."

"Does Mom know your job is so dangerous?" Annie asked him.

"This is the exception to the rule," Dad said.

"So what do you normally do?" Abbie asked him.

He shrugged.

"I don't know. Look for stolen purses. Help with citizens' disputes. That sort of thing."

"How often is the job like this?" I asked as we rounded a curve.

I looked at the speedometer. We were going one hundred twenty.

"Not often," he said.

In the distance I could see a sign.

It was a welcome sign. Welcoming drivers into the next state.

"I'll never get them before we hit the next state," my dad muttered.

"But you'll stick with them. Right?" Abbie asked.

"I'd hate to think they get off the hook for slipping into the next state," Annie added.

"If that were the case, I bet there'd be a lot of robberies near state borders," I mentioned.

"Not to mention, we need to save Mrs. Farnsworth," Annie finished.

"We're not going to let them go," my dad said. "But we *do* need some help."

"From the Feds?" I asked.

"Yes," he replied. "They can pursue things over state lines."

I nodded. "I get it."

"Good thing I gassed up before I picked you guys up from school," he said.

Abbie snorted a laugh.

"Can you imagine?! Being on a car chase and running out of gas?" she said with another laugh.

"I'm sure it's happened," Annie replied.

"Let's hope it doesn't happen here," I mentioned.

"Let's hope," my dad added.

Just then I heard what sounded like eggbeaters.

Not the ones you eat. You know, the yellow eggs that are only egg whites. Sold in tiny little cartons. But the ones like my grandmother uses to beat eggs.

It's a funny-looking device. It's got a handle and these two things on the end. Like the things you stick into an electric mixer.

Pfft, pfft, pfft, pfft, pfft.

We looked overhead.

It was a helicopter.

"Is that the Feds?" I asked my dad.

He looked up. But only quickly.

At these speeds, he had to keep his eyes on the road.

"No," he said. "It's a TV station."

Abbie got all excited.

"We're going to be on *TV*?" she shrieked with pleasure.

Just then it hit all four of us at the same time.

"Oh, no!" we all said at once.

"You think they can see us?" Annie asked.

My father nodded slowly. "Yup."

"So everyone will know we're in the car with you?" Abbie added.

My father nodded heavily. "Yup."

"Will you get into trouble at work?" I asked him.

My father nodded again. "Yup."

Great. Just great.

Abbie took a comb from her backpack and started combing her hair.

"What are you *doing*?!" I asked her.

"Looking good for my public," she replied.

"You have '*public*?'" Annie asked.

"Yeah. Who do you think you are?! Paris Hilton?" I snorted a laugh.

Abbie made a face. "Ugh. No *way*! Who'd want to be Paris Hilton?!"

You'd figure my father would be coming undone about now. Possibly even telling us to be quiet.

I mean, the discussion *was* a little stupid.

But strangely? He seemed pleased by the exchange.

His eyes flicked at the rearview mirror. Toward Abbie.

"You wouldn't want to be Paris Hilton?" he asked Abbie.

She made a face. One that registered disgust.

"God, no!" she effused.

Dad smiled widely. "Why not?" he asked.

Personally? I figured, *who cared*?!

But it seemed my dad did.

"Because…" Abbie thought about it for a few seconds.

We were speeding after the bank robbers. Lights flashing. Sirens wailing.

Helicopters were hovering above us.

Recording every mile. Every turn. Every *bump*!

But here? Inside this car? It seemed the only important thing to my dad? Was the answer Abbie was about to give.

CHAPTER 7

"I don't know," Abbie started. "She's not what she should be."

"What do you mean?" my dad asked her as if we were on a Sunday drive in the country. And not on a speeding car chase. With gun-toting bank robbers.

"I think that someone with *her* money," Abbie started.

"And her *advantage* in life," Annie continued.

"Should be a *lot* more of a positive influence," I finished.

"Yeah," Abbie said. "That's *exactly* what I mean."

My father was glowing.

"I couldn't agree with you more," he said proudly.

We all thought about that.

"What would you guys do if you *had* all her money?" my dad asked us.

"I'd help homeless orphans," Annie said. "All over the world."

Yup. That was Annie all right.

"And you?" my dad asked Abbie.

She had to think about that for a few seconds.

"I know," she said. "I'd start my own fashion line. And I'd buy my own mountain. With a year-round snow blower! That way I could go skiing *every* day of the year."

Okay. So that was like Abbie.

"And you, Andrew?" my dad asked me.

That was an easy one!

"I'd buy up all the schools. Then I'd shut them down," I said proudly.

Hey. Annie wasn't the *only* one who cared about people! I had a big heart too, you know.

Abbie rolled her eyes at me. She was giving me her best "You're an idiot" look.

"Either that?" I added. "Or I'd buy myself a football team."

My dad laughed.

"With all her money? You could probably do both," he said with a chuckle.

The pfft, pfft, pfft, pfft sound got louder. Like it had an echo or something.

I glanced out my window, and looked up.

Now there were two helicopters up there.

"*That's* the Feds," my dad told us.

I was surprised. "Wow," I said. "That's *huge*."

My dad nodded. "It's a search and rescue bird," he explained. "An HC 60."

There was a big plane flying nearby.

"What's that?" I asked my dad.

"What?" he asked.

"That big plane," I said, pointing.

47

The road was winding a bit. So he couldn't take his eyes off of it.

"I can't look now," he said. "But it's probably a C-130."

"What's a C-130?" I asked.

"Does it look like a fat bird?" he asked. "Kind of chubby?"

"Yes," Annie said. "It *does*."

"Then it's a C-130. The C-130 can be used as a transport vehicle. But it's also used like a tanker. It holds gas for the helicopters," my dad explained.

"How do they get it from the plane to the helicopter?" Annie asked.

"Do they have to land?" Abbie asked.

"Or can they do it in the air?" I asked.

My dad chuckled. "There's a pipe on the C-130. It gets longer. Like a telescope. Or an antenna."

The road swerved to the left. And we were dodging afternoon drivers like ants. But my dad kept up with the robbers.

"Anyhow," he said as the road straightened a bit. "They extend the pipe. Then they hook it to the bird."

"In midair?" I asked.

"Yes," he nodded.

"That's *way* cool!" I said.

"I hope we get to see it," Annie said.

"I hope we don't," Dad voiced.

"Why not?" Abbie asked.

48

"Because that'll mean we've been doing this for a while," Dad said.

"We've already *been* doing this for a while," Abbie pointed out.

"Anything more than five *minutes* is a 'while' to you," I said to Abbie.

"Why don't you shut up," she spit at me.

"Why don't *you* shut up?" I spat back.

"Why don't you *both* shut up?!" Annie and my father said in unison.

The radio started to crackle.

"Alpha nine nine three. Come in Alpha nine nine three."

It was Gert.

My dad pointed to the radio thing.

Annie handed it to him.

"Alpha nine nine three here," my dad said into the radio thing.

"We're watching you on the news, Alpha nine nine three," she said.

"How *cool*!" Abbie gushed. "We're on the news!"

"Are you *forgetting* something, dimwit?" I asked her.

"Shut up, *moron*." Abbie threw me a dirty look.

"Why don't *you* shut up," I threw right back at her.

"Not *now*, kids," my father warned.

"Alpha nine nine three," Gert stated. "We have your wife on the line."

All squabbling stopped.

In its place was a collective gasp.

"Oh, dang!" I said.

"Mom's on the line," Annie added.

"I guess she caught us on TV," Abbie finished.

My father groaned loudly.

"This is going to be bad," I mumbled.

"Very bad," Annie added.

"The *worst*," Abbie finished.

My father groaned again.

"Alpha nine nine three? Are you still there?" Gert asked.

All I could think was: *not for long!*

Bringing us on an interstate police car chase? When his only job was to pick us up from school and take us home?

He thought he'd be in trouble from *work*?!

They could do *nothing* to him! *Nothing*!

Maybe fire him. At the *worst*.

But when my *mom* got her hands on him? After *this* fiasco?!

Well, let's just say…

My dad was dead meat.

"Yes, control. I'm still here," he said with dread.

"Your wife wants to know if those other passengers in your car are her children," Gert said gently.

Wow. The wording said it all.

When Mom called us "her" children? She was *really* mad at Dad.

My father was at a loss for words.

"Alpha nine nine three. Did you copy?" Gert asked.

Yeah, I'd have to say Dad "copied" all right. His face was as white as a ghost.

"Ohhh," I said out loud. "*That's* where I've seen the driver's mask before! He's Casper!"

"Oh, right," Annie added. "He's Casper the ghost."

"The *friendly* ghost," Abbie finished.

And speaking about being finished?

Put a fork in Dad.

'Cause he was *done*!

CHAPTER 8

"Your mother's going to kill me," Dad said sadly.

"No she won't, Dad," Annie said gently.

"Yes," Abbie said. "She will."

"Maybe not," I offered.

"We'll just tell her the truth," Annie said.

"That you *were* taking us home," Abbie added.

"When we almost got creamed by the robbers," I finished.

My father stepped on the gas to keep up with the Impala.

"Oh yes. *That's* a good excuse," he said with sorrow.

"You'll see," Annie said. "Everything will work out."

"That's right, Dad," Abbie added.

"It always does," I finished.

Abbie made a face. "Well, not *always*."

Dad looked dejected.

"Would you *please* shut up?!" I snapped at Abbie.

"*You* shut up," Abbie countered.

"Don't you two ever get tired of that?" Annie asked Abbie and me.

"I know *I* do," my dad said.

The radio crackled.

"Alpha nine nine three?" Gert said.

Annie handed Dad the radio thing.

"Yes, control?"

Gert coughed into the radio. "Ah. Your wife wants to know how her children are doing."

"They're all fine," Dad said.

Then he looked at us. As if to make sure he was right.

"I'm great," Annie said.

"Me, too," Abbie added.

"It's all good," I finished.

Dad kind of smiled.

Overhead we heard lots of whirring.

"You've got three TV stations and the FBI above you," Gert said.

"Wow," Annie said.

"*Three* TV stations?!" Abbie gushed.

"Cool!" I added.

"Any units nearby?" Dad asked.

He was asking about other police cars.

Maybe if other units were nearby, he could just take us home. Possibly get out of the doghouse. You know, with Mom.

But then he wouldn't get his arrests.

I mean, we'd come so far. And were so close. It would be a shame if he didn't finish the job.

"No," Gert said. "Just you, Alpha nine nine three."

"Where are all the local cars?" Dad asked Gert.

"Keeping people off the entrance ramps," Gert

informed us.

"I *thought* the highway was looking less and less crowded," Dad commented.

"No one wants any civilians to get hurt," Gert said.

"Me neither," Dad agreed.

In the radio's background I could hear someone sort of screaming.

I couldn't make out the words. It sounded like Charlie Brown's teacher. Like a sad trombone. With a plunger stuck in it.

You know. *Whah, whah, whah, whah.*

"Um. Alpha nine nine three?"

"Yes, Gert?"

"Your wife wants to know something," she said softly.

Here it comes. I could feel it.

Dad visibly braced himself.

"Go ahead," he said to Gert.

"Well, ah. She wants to know why—if you didn't want to hurt any civilians—you brought her children on this police chase."

Annie grabbed the radio thing.

"Tell Mom we're all fine," she said into the thing.

Abbie coached Annie from the back seat. "Tell her it wasn't Dad's fault."

"It's not Dad's fault," Annie repeated into the thing.

"That it was *your* fault," I instructed Annie.

Annie wailed into the radio thing. "It was all *my*

fault," she confessed.

"Explain why," Abbie said to Annie.

"If I hadn't freed the frogs? *None* of this would've happened."

Annie was crying now.

My father looked frustrated.

"Don't cry, honey. This is *not* your fault," he said.

"Yes it is," Abbie and I rebuked.

Annie cried harder "It's *all my fault*," she yowled into the radio thing.

My dad leaned over and took the radio thing from her hand.

"Give me that!" he said.

He barked into the radio thing.

"Gert! Please tell my wife I'm a little *busy* right now!"

Annie was crying loudly.

"I'm chasing perps. Who have a hostage! At *three* digit speeds!" he spit out.

He was at his limit about now.

"I made the *dumb* mistake of putting Abbie and Andrew together in the back seat," he added.

Sweat was beading on his forehead. And that vein was pulsing like mad again.

"They've been bickering *nonstop* through this *entire* chase!" he yelled.

Oh, yeah. He was at his limit all right.

"And now *Annie's* crying," he ended his tirade.

Now that that was said? He was beginning to calm

down a little.

"So you can see why I have my hands full at the moment," he said.

He sounded a little calmer.

"Please tell all of that to my wife," he muttered quietly.

I think he was a little embarrassed. You know, for losing it like that.

Gert cleared her throat.

"Will do, Alpha nine nine three," she said.

"Thank you," my dad said kindly.

The storm was over.

At least *that* one was.

Little did we know.

We? The Leegs? Were headed right for another one.

CHAPTER 9

It started to rain.

"Oh. This is just wonderful," my father said.

"At least we're inside," Annie said through her sniffles.

"And it's only raining lightly," Abbie added.

I knew she was trying to make amends. You know, for the trouble she'd caused mere minutes before.

I felt sorry for my dad.

"Very lightly," I pointed out.

"That's the trouble," my dad said.

He flipped on the windshield wipers.

"A harder rain would be safer," he said.

I didn't get that.

"Why?" I asked.

"Yeah," Abbie said. "You can still see everything."

"It's not the windshield I'm worried about," he explained. "It's the road."

"But the road's barely wet," I said.

He nodded.

"This is more hazardous than a stronger rain," he said.

I still wasn't getting it.

Obviously neither was Annie.

"Why?" she asked.

"Because the road turns slick," he said.

"Slicker than if it's more wet?" Abbie asked.

She didn't look convinced.

Dad nodded.

"The slight water, mixed with the oil on the road? It's very dangerous," he explained.

Annie nodded. "I get it. It makes the road like a sheet of ice."

"Oh," I said. "Like an oil slick."

My dad nodded.

"It's especially dangerous at these speeds," he said nervously.

We were on a curve. A deep curve.

As if the Impala had heard my dad, it slid sideways.

Off the road.

Well, it hadn't really slid *sideways*. It kept going straight while the road turned.

My dad tried to slow the police car down.

"I can't slam on the brakes," he said.

He was pumping them. Gently.

We followed the Impala as best we could.

Luckily, though, we stopped.

The Impala also stopped.

Right into a road sign.

It almost sliced the Impala in half.

Three doors opened quickly. Casper, Barney, Mrs.

Farnsworth and Ax-head all jumped out.

Casper tugged at Mrs. Farnsworth.

Then they started to run in three different directions.

Hm. The robbers were smarter than they looked.

Actually, they looked pretty stupid.

Dad swore under his breath. "They're taking Mrs. Farnsworth!"

"Well, *Casper* is," I noted.

"So the other two will get away?" Annie muttered with shock.

"Looks that way," my dad said with frustration.

Abbie looked at Annie and me.

"Oh no they *won't*," she said to Dad.

We all knew what we had to do.

"I'll take Ax-head," I said.

"I'll take Casper," Annie added.

"And I'll take Barney," Abbie finished.

We all took off for our assigned robbers.

"I can't *wait* to kick Barney's butt. Been wanting to do that for *years*!" Abbie said as she set out.

Naturally, my father freaked.

"*NO!*" he called out to us. "*Stop!* It's too dangerous!"

"Help Annie and Mrs. Farnsworth," I yelled to him over my shoulder.

Then I disappeared into the woods. Right behind Ax-head.

I wondered if he had a gun.

I wondered if he'd use it.

The leaves were off the trees. And he was leaving a trail that was *very* easy to follow.

He must drag his feet or something.

Ahead, I heard a thud and a grunt. It sounded like Ax-head hit a tree.

I said nothing.

I didn't want him to know how close I was.

He was feeling around for something. And kept turning his head around. Like he was trying to see where I was.

His hands kept sweeping the area close to him.

But he came up with nothing.

I was now only about fifteen feet behind him. But I stood quietly.

I figured it was best not to let him know I was so near.

But you know how all good plans go wrong?

Well, *mine* always did.

All of a sudden I sneezed. It was a loud sneeze.

But I didn't expect the reaction I got from him.

I expected him to turn on me.

To come *at* me.

To attack.

But he didn't.

Instead, he jumped.

Like I'd scared him. Out of his wits!

He hopped up and started running again.

So I took off after him again.

For my Dad's sake, I couldn't lose him. My dad

needed the collar.

I had no idea what I was going to *do* with him once I caught him.

But the *least* I could do was keep *up* with him.

When I got to the tree? I saw it.

A shiny object.

Laying amongst the leaves.

I dove for it. Quickly. Scooping it up as I ran.

Then I looked at it while I was still running.

Hm. What do you know?! It was a gun.

A big gun. A shiny gun.

A big, shiny gun.

And now it was mine.

Which probably meant…

He was unarmed.

I mean, how many weapons could he have brought on this little jog?

Not many.

They hadn't planned for this, I'm sure.

They hadn't even had time to take off their masks after the *robbery*!

We'd been all over them before they could change out of their robbery-wear.

So, I thought as I ran my butt off. *I've got you. And I've got your gun too!*

The guy was starting to tire. I could tell.

I could hear him wheezing.

Guess he didn't expect to be chased down by Andrew

61

Leeg.

He was slowing down a little.

I wasn't.

Seems the track team had served me well.

CHAPTER 10

His wheezing worsened.

"You should quit while you're ahead," I called to him. "Even if it *does* have an ax in it."

The guy didn't laugh. I don't know *why*. *I* thought it was funny.

"So where you be-headed?" I called to him.

He kept running.

"*Beheaded*?" I repeated. "Get it?"

Nothing.

"Aw come on!" I called to him. "That's funny!"

A helicopter flew above us.

"Don't look now," I called to the guy I was chasing. "But we have company."

The guy just kept on running.

"Know why I said 'don't look now'? Because I didn't want you to take your *eye* off of where you were going," I called after him.

He veered to the left.

So did I.

"Get it?" I said. "Your one *good* eye?"

The guy was wheezing heavily now.

He was really slowing down.

I decided to make my move.

I was still holding onto his gun.

"Yo. Buddy. Why don't you stop now," I suggested. "You're not much ahead anymore."

He kept on going.

"Get it? Not much of a *head* anymore?"

Total silence.

Except for the wheezing. Which was getting worse.

"You really should stop," I said "You sound awful."

I hadn't really expected him to stop.

I mean, what robber, in their right mind, would stop because someone told them to?

But weirdly? He stopped.

I waved his gun at him.

"I've got you covered," I said.

"And we have you in plain view," the helicopter's loudspeaker blared.

A man was leaning out of the chopper. He had a huge video camera stuck to his eye.

The lens was tremendous.

It was obviously one of the TV stations.

"We've got you live and on the air," someone said over the loudspeaker. "For this late breaking news exclusive."

Ax-head threw his hands up.

I steadied the gun on him. Even though the helicopter was blowing wind all over the place.

Then the Federal bird flew into view.

"Do you have a capture here?" its loudspeaker blared.

I nodded. "Sure do," I said.

"Good work, kid," the voice called down to me.

Just then a man fluttered down from the chopper. He was on a moving rope or something.

When he landed right next to me, I smiled.

"That's cool," I said.

"It's called a winch. We use it for search and rescue missions," he explained.

He took out a pair of handcuffs.

"Turn around, please," he said to Ax-head.

Ax-head did as he was told. His head hung down low.

Then the Federal guy looped something around Ax-head's body a few times.

After he tugged it a few times, he held his thumb up. Then he pumped it skyward.

Within milliseconds, Ax-head was floating upwards.

"You did a great job, son," the man said to me. "What's your name?"

"Andrew. Andrew Leeg."

He nodded. "You must be the officer's kid."

"Yeah. That's my dad," I said. "Do you know where he is?"

The guy nodded. "He and some girl are chasing down Casper the ghost."

"Still?" I asked.

The guy nodded.

"The ghost must be in better shape than Ax-head

here," I said with a grin.

The guy smiled and nodded.

"That, and he's armed and has a hostage. So your dad's being cautious," he said. "That's wise."

He held his hand to his helmet, and leaned a little.

"Hey," he said. "We've got to go. It seems *another* kid has caught Barney."

I nodded. "That's my sister. Abbie."

The guy grinned. "Well apparently, your sister Abbie is kicking the, ah, crud out of Barney."

"Yeah. That sounds like her. She really hates Barney."

The guy laughed.

The winch slid back down and the guy snapped himself on.

Then he grabbed me at the last minute, and lifted me up with him.

I was scared like you wouldn't believe.

"Look, Mom," I said. "No hands!"

The guy with the camera in the TV chopper laughed.

"That was great!" he called to me. "I got it on camera!"

Oh no! Now my mom really *would* see it!

My dad was totally in the doghouse now!

When we got up to the bay of the helicopter, I was shocked.

"It's so roomy in here," I said.

"Plenty of room to get Barney, your sister Abbie, Casper, the hostage and your dad," the man said to me with a chuckle.

"And don't forget my other sister," I said. "Annie."

"Oh yes. And her too."

That gave me a thought. "If you're going to leave anyone behind, try to make it Abbie. Okay?"

The guy cracked up. "Will do, son."

"Thanks," I said.

"But we never leave a man behind," he said seriously.

I understood. But just in case *he* didn't, I thought I'd explain.

"We're triplets," I said to him. "And I can handle Annie okay. It's Abbie who's the evil one."

He motioned for me to buckle up.

"There's always an evil one," he said as I clicked in.

The bird banked to the right. Hard.

I was afraid Ax-head would fall out of the open side.

Obviously he was too. Because he was screaming his head off. But he was latched in.

"Pipe down, One-eye," another Federal guy said to him.

"We call him Ax-head," my Federal guy said to his teammate as he pointed between himself and me.

We all cracked up.

Well, all of us except for One-eye Ax-head.

"That's a really stupid disguise," the Federal guy said.

"And I bet it's hot in there," another commented.

"Wait till you see Barney!" I noted.

That brought big laughs.

Chapter 11

We swooped around again.

I was glad I hadn't eaten lunch. I would've lost it.

One of the guys by the door started to laugh.

He was pointing at the ground below.

Everyone else went to the doorway to see what was so funny.

I stayed on my side of the helicopter. Afraid it would tip over like a boat.

And then crash.

"That's hilarious," one guy said.

"Is that a *girl*?" another one asked.

"Looks like it," a third said.

I inched over to the doorway. Still afraid the mass movement would get us killed.

Maybe if I moved *slowly*, the pilot could compensate. You know, for the shift in load.

My head barely got over the point where I could see out.

"That's my sister Abbie," I said.

Everyone barked a laugh at what they'd just seen.

"Wow. Did you catch *that* last move?!" one of the guys cried out.

"She's opening a can of whoop—"

Before the guy could finish his sentence, we dove downward. Although it didn't matter. We all knew—including me—what kind of can Abbie was opening up.

I didn't just *know* it. I'd been on the *receiving* end of it. A time or two.

Or a million.

"Get the ears," someone yelled.

A big round dish was passed to the doorway.

It looked like one of those satellite dishes.

"Put it on speaker," another guy yelled.

A cord was passed from the dish to the front of the chopper.

The co-pilot made a motion with his hand.

"Turn it on, Luke," another guy shouted.

And the chopper's cabin was instantly filled with the sounds of Abbie.

"Move it, *dirt bag*!" she yelled at the purple dinosaur.

The guys all broke out in laughter.

"I'm going as fast as I can," the dinosaur wailed.

"No wonder you're extinct," she hollered at him. "You move with the speed and grace of a *dump truck*!"

The guys were cracking up again.

"Wow. She's *vicious*!" one said with a chuckle.

"Tell me about it!" I commented. "She's my sister!"

A mass groan came from many of the men.

"Ew," one said. "I feel for you, man."

"She's a lot like *my* sister was," another said.

69

"Good luck to ya, kid," yet another said.

Abbie could be heard screaming, "Left. Left. Left, right, left!"

Our attention was back on Abbie.

"Pick up those stupid feet," she barked.

One of the guys laughed. "She *is* kind of funny."

"Yeah," I said. "Until she's got it out for *you*."

The guy grunted in response. I think he was agreeing with me. Especially when we all heard the next thing she said.

"And watch where you're going, *dufus*!" she yelled loudly.

"It's hard to see in this stupid mask," Barney tried to explain.

But Abbie wasn't hearing any excuses.

"So?" Abbie said back to the robber. "That's *my* problem?!"

We were hovering right above Abbie and her captive.

"I can get down there okay now," one of the rescuers said. "But it would be easier if they were out from the trees."

"Just tell Abbie," I told the guy. "She'll get him wherever you want him."

"She *does* seem in control of the situation," he said.

"She's in control of *all* situations," I informed him.

"But what if the guy messes with her?" he asked me.

That made me laugh.

The rescue guy still looked nervous. "He *did* just pull

a bank heist."

Below, Barney must have stopped walking.

"Don't make me stop, purple-boy!" Abbie warned the robber. "Or I just *may* have the time to hurt you."

The guys all cracked up.

"Look," one shouted and pointed. "Barney's started walking again."

"And his pace is *quite* peppy," another observed before they all started laughing.

The rescue guy was no longer worried. Abbie could obviously take care of herself.

"Where do you want her to go?" I asked the man.

"About two hundred feet west," he said.

"Have a speaker?" I asked him.

Someone passed me a bullhorn.

I turned it on and the feedback was deafening.

"Whoa," I said. "Sorry."

"No problem," the guys said with a hearty laugh.

I guess everyone did that, and they saw it coming.

I tried it again. Only this time, with the satellite dish thing faced the other way.

"Abbie?" I called to her.

She looked up quickly.

"It's me, Andrew," I said.

She made a face.

You didn't need a satellite listening dish to tell you what *that* face meant.

A loose translation? *I know that, ditwad!*

A tighter translation? *What the heck do you want, moron?! Can't you see that I'm busy?*

"The guys want you to go two hundred feet west," I said.

She made another face.

And added a hand gesture.

The guys laughed.

"Yup. She is *exactly* like my sister used to be," the guy with the sister like Abbie commented.

"I noticed you said 'used to be,'" I said. "Did you kill her?"

All the guys cracked up.

"Nope," he said kindly. "She grew out of it."

At first I thought, *Oh, good. So there's hope.*

But then I heard another guy say, "No she didn't!"

That made everyone roar with laughter.

I didn't get the joke.

"What's so funny?" I asked.

The guy with the sister like Abbie was laughing so hard, tears were rolling down his cheeks.

"What's so *funny*?!" I asked again.

"That's Mike. My brother-in-law," he said between bouts of laughter.

"So?" I asked.

"He married… my sister."

Loud roars could be heard throughout the chopper.

Once they'd died down, the man added, "Mike and I used to be best friends."

He looked at the man who married his sister.

"Not any *more!*" Mike said with fake anger.

All the guys cracked up again.

So I guess I was out of luck. You know, as far as Abbie growing out of her personality.

But meanwhile? She was giving Barney the purple dinosaur a real butt kicking.

I knew he deserved it, so I hated to make it stop. But I had to tell Abbie to get him to a clearing.

"Abbie," I called through the bullhorn.

"What?!" she screamed back.

One of the guys took the bullhorn.

"We need you to turn left," he said.

When she heard it was someone else? She immediately listened.

Me? I could've said the same thing, and she'd ignore me.

In fact, I *did* say the same thing. And she'd flipped me the bird!

She turned left.

And poked Barney with a long stick. That forced him to turn left, too.

"That's great, Abbie," the guy said.

She looked up quickly and smiled. One of her big flashy smiles.

For a moment there, she looked all sweet and innocent.

But I knew better.

And so did Barney.

And so did the rescue guys.

She wasn't kidding *anyone*.

"Take your prisoner about two hundred feet. Straight ahead," the man instructed her.

She kept on hiking. Through the trees.

Prodding Barney all the way.

Chapter 12

She got to the clearing right as we were landing.

She was still poking Barney with that stick.

"*Move it, maggot!*" she screamed at him.

Poor guy must've been as purple on the inside as he was on the outside.

Pretty purple.

Not pretty purple like, "Ew, that's a pretty purple." But pretty purple like *really* black and blue.

"Great job, Abbie," one of the guys said as he hopped out the chopper's doorway.

He cuffed Barney and tossed him next to Ax-head.

Then they hooked Barney to the chopper, too.

Just like they'd done with Ax-head. So they couldn't escape. Or fall out of the bird.

"Okay," Abbie said loudly. "Casper's next. Let's go get him!"

She was all pumped up.

"Aren't you satisfied with getting *your* prisoner?" I asked her.

I mean, *I'd* gotten Ax-head and was satisfied with *that*.

"Bring me to Casper and *bring... him... on!*" Abbie

roared.

I looked at the guy who had a sister like Abbie.

"*Sis*," he called softly so just I could hear.

But Mike (his brother-in-law) had other ideas of entertainment.

"Yes, dear," he said blandly.

Everyone cracked up. Including me this time.

Well, everyone but Abbie.

She hadn't even noticed.

She was now sticking her twig at both Barney *and* Ax-head.

The pilot called back to us.

"We have the location of the third thief."

"Bring him on!" Abbie repeated.

I looked at my sister. "You've *got* to stop drinking those power drinks," I told her.

She'd won a ski competition this past winter. And the sponsors—a power drink company—gave her a lifetime supply of their product.

I think she was trying to drink the entire lifetime supply in a few months. It was like she was addicted to the stuff. And I wasn't sure, but I think it made her even *more* aggressive than she usually was.

The chopper turned sharply.

"Does my dad have his guy in custody?" I asked. "And how's Mrs. Farnsworth?"

They passed the message up to the pilot.

I saw him on his radio thing.

He turned and gave the message back. It went through a bunch of guys before I got it.

I wondered if it were like playing telephone as a kid.

You remember that. Don't you? You know. You start with one kid in class? And it spreads through the whole classroom?

But by the time it got to the last person? It was *totally* different.

I had a second-grade teacher who wanted us to have better listening skills. So we played telephone.

She said that if we could get the sentence exactly as she said it? We could have an extra half hour of recess.

In second grade? That was pretty darned great! It was like offering free iPods.

Anyhow, out of the whole school year? We only got an extra half hour of recess twice!

Yeah, that's right. Only twice!

We renamed the game after that.

We didn't call it "playing telephone" anymore. We called it "kill the guy at the end!"

Let's just say, nobody wanted to be the guy at the end.

But getting back to here and now...

I wondered how "off" the message would be.

"Your father and sister have not caught their guy yet. But they've been keeping up with him," was the message.

In school? That would have been: "Your father said

your sister should be on a diet. But that was before she ate him."

Truth be told?

These guys were pretty good at playing telephone.

Where were *they* when I was in second grade?!

The helicopter rounded another turn.

I could catch glimpses of Annie's pink t-shirt.

My dad was right behind her. But he was harder to see in his navy blue uniform.

I kept my eye on the pink t-shirt.

I looked for Casper and Mrs. Farnsworth. They were about fifteen feet ahead of Dad and Annie.

It was plain to see what was happening. Casper was holding a gun on Mrs. Farnsworth.

So my dad and sister were being very cautious.

We watched from above.

All four helicopters were now in a small area.

It was getting mighty crowded up here.

"Tell those media hounds to back off!" one of the guys said.

The pilot got on his radio.

Two minutes later he turned around.

He shook his head and shrugged.

The guy who'd barked the command was ticked off.

He got up and stormed to the cockpit. (Or whatever it's called on a helicopter.)

He grabbed the radio thing from the pilot's hand.

"*Clear… this… airspace!*" he roared into it.

The other choppers kept their places.

The man's face turned very red.

"Tell them you'll give the first one who clears out of here an exclusive," someone shouted aloud.

"And the other two will be shot down!" someone else added.

That got the guys roaring with laughter.

But the red-faced man liked the idea.

"The first to leave and land will get an exclusive interview. With the robbers, the police, the rescue team *and* the kids," he barked into the radio thing.

"And what will the rest of us get?" one of the TV pilots asked.

"Shot!"

Funny, but they all took off.

The guys roared with laughter again.

For a bunch of guys who did something so serious? They sure were a happy bunch!

They looked out the doorway and the windows.

"I can't see who's going to land first," one of the guys said.

"That's not our problem," the red-faced man said as he came back to our area. "Let them duke it out."

"Meanwhile," another guy said. "We've now got clear airspace."

"To do our thang!" another guy added.

"Pony up," red-faced man said.

A few of the guys stood up and started shoving a bunch of stuff in their jumpsuits.

"What's all that?" I asked.

"Stuff we may need," one answered.

Someone ripped a big piece of paper off what looked like a printer. Then he handed it to one of the guys.

The guy started folding it up tightly.

"What kind of stuff?" I asked.

"Compass. Weapons. Maps," one of the guys said.

"First aid supplies. Meds. Food," another added.

"You name it," the first guy said.

"We've probably got it," the second guy said.

I could tell they were a team. They thought alike. They finished each other's sentences.

That's a good thing, I suppose, if you're a team. Doing dangerous work like these guys did.

"Ready to go in?" one asked.

"Just say the word," a few of them said.

"'The word,'" the first guy said with a smile. "Okay. On three."

They all snapped on a few things and shuffled to their places.

"One."

"Two."

"*Three.*"

And like bats in the dusk? They flew out the open door of the helicopter.

CHAPTER 13

We watched from above.

It was totally cool!

The guys went down the winch thing quickly. One on the end of it, and the others sliding down the wire.

They landed on the ground quickly.

I watched as they moved silently through the woods.

Not speaking.

Just doing.

It was as if they'd rehearsed the thing a thousand times before.

I had no idea how they were doing what they were doing.

They *did* give each other hand signals. But I hadn't a clue what they meant.

Yet they did.

I followed their movements with awe.

They ended up passing my dad and sister Annie.

They moved stealthily around the robber and Mrs. Farnsworth.

No one even *knew* they were in the woods.

They surpassed the robber and Mrs. Farnsworth.

Wow. If *anyone* was ghostlike? It wasn't Casper the

thieving ghost! It was *those* guys.

"Wow," I whispered to myself.

A man behind me clapped my back. "Pretty awesome, huh?"

"They're amazing!" I answered.

"We've got the best PJs in the country," he said proudly.

I looked at the guy.

I looked at his jumpsuit.

"They're PJs?" I asked.

The guy laughed.

"No. This is a flight suit, son. I'm not talking about pajamas."

"Oh," I said, embarrassed.

"PJs are para-jumpers," he explained.

"Like guys who *jump* with *parachutes*," another said.

"But our guys also scuba dive and mountain climb!" the first guy added.

"That is *way* cool!" I said.

The guys nodded.

"And these guys are the best. So don't worry about your dad, your sister or the hostage," the first guy said.

"Or *your* little friend," the second guy said to Ax-head and Barney.

"They'll get them all," the first guy assured Abbie and me.

As if on cue, Casper the friendly ghost showed up at the doorway. He was strapped to the winch.

The guys on board untied him.

Then they handcuffed him and stuck him with his friends.

"It's coming down again," a guy called downward.

They sent the winch back down.

A few moments later, Mrs. Farnsworth came up.

She was a little flustered. But she was okay. And safe.

Then Dad and Annie came up together.

We were all so busy hugging that we missed the return of the PJs.

"Another fine job," the red-faced man said with a smile.

The rest of the guys all cheered.

"So what would you like to do?" the red-faced man asked my dad.

"Can my kids and I come with you?" Dad asked.

"Sure," the red-faced man said.

"Can you take us to the precinct?"

"Sure," he said with a grin.

He threw his thumb at Barney, Ax-head and Casper.

"You'll have to book these clowns."

My dad smiled. "Three collars," he said with excitement.

"You did a fine job, officer," the red-faced man said.

"Thank you, Colonel," my dad said back.

"And I see your children are part of your team," the Colonel added.

My dad looked at the three of us. "The best part," he

said proudly.

We got back to the precinct quickly. Landed in the parking lot.

Lots of people came running out of the precinct. They all wanted to hear about the capture firsthand.

But for Dad? Business came before pleasure.

First he took the three robbers inside.

He fingerprinted them, took their pictures, and booked them.

"Good job, Leeg," my dad's boss blustered.

"Thank you, sir," my dad answered.

"At first I was a little flummoxed about why you took your children," he admitted.

My dad turned to looked at us and winked.

"But as they say. All is well that ends well, I suppose," Dad's boss declared.

"Which reminds me," my father said. "I need another officer to go with me to the crash site."

"What for?" his boss crowed. "We have the criminals. *And* the hostage."

"I need to pick up the squad car," my dad said to his boss.

His boss nodded.

"And also something else," my dad muttered under his breath.

Officer Mahoney volunteered to go with Dad. They were good friends, so Dad took him.

"Don't go anywhere!" Dad said to Abbie, Annie and

me.

Gert ran right for us. "Don't worry. I'll watch them," she said happily.

"Okay, Gert," Dad said with a smile. "Thanks."

"Want some doughnuts?" Gert asked us as soon as my dad left the room.

The minute my dad drove away, all heck broke loose.

All three TV stations arrived for their "exclusive" interview.

They'd realized they'd been stood up. And figured the Federal guys would drop everyone back here. After all. This was the town where the robbery had taken place.

"*We* get the exclusive," one blond woman said.

"No. *We* do!" another blond woman argued.

"You're *both* wrong," a man with a plastic smile said simply. "*I* get the interview."

They were fighting like cats and dogs.

Or raging bulls.

Or triplets.

"You get your hair color from a bottle!" one blond said to the other.

"You get your *nourishment* from a bottle!" the other one threw back.

The man with the plastic smile stepped in. "Ladies, ladies, *please*."

I don't know. I may be wrong. But that was probably the *worst* thing he could've said or done.

They turned on him like jackals!

"Stay out of this, *plastic hair*!" the one who drinks said to the man.

The bleached blond was even more cruel. "That's not plastic, Anita. It's a *rug*!"

They cackled like two witches around a cauldron.

"Ladies we're live in three… two… one," a man said from behind a big video camera.

During the countdown, the two blond ladies and the plastic man scurried to separate corners.

"And good evening, ladies and gentlemen," they each said.

"Welcome to the five o'clock news," they almost said in unison.

Then they introduced themselves.

After that? It was like a free for all.

The two blondes and the man started grabbing at people. Particularly, Mrs. Farnsworth. Asking all sorts of questions.

"Were you afraid?"

"When did you know about the robbery?"

"How much did they get?"

"Who was the arresting officer?"

"Were any lives lost in the incident?"

"Why were there children involved in the chase?"

Right after that *last* question?

That's when things got *really* bad.

CHAPTER 14

As soon as someone mentioned that we were the arresting officer's kids? The three of them clawed at us.

Each one trying to grab one of us.

The drinker grabbed Annie's arm.

Annie cried out.

I didn't know if it was in pain or surprise.

But either way? That lady wasn't going to get away with it!

"Get your hands off my sister!" I shouted into the camera.

The woman recoiled as if she'd been slapped.

I guess having yourself made to seem evil on live TV had that effect on the woman.

"I-I-I wasn't going to hurt her," she stammered. On live TV.

"Why don't you *ask* someone," Annie said to her.

"If you want to *speak* with them," I added coldly.

"Instead of just *grabbing* and *pulling*," Abbie finished.

The woman just stood there with her mouth hanging open.

Her perfectly-lipsticked mouth.

Just hanging open.

Catching flies.

The other blond lady took that as her chance.

"Oh *chil*dren," she trilled.

Children?

Who did she think we were? Hansel and Gretel? And another Gretel?

We turned to face her.

"Would you like… to speak… with… *me-ee*?" she asked.

She sounded like she was talking to two year olds.

"Not particularly," we all said in unison.

Then we laughed.

So did the plastic guy.

I kind of felt sorry for him.

He was stuck competing with those two women. I knew how he felt.

I too had to sometimes wear a plastic smile when I was with my sisters.

Maybe he wasn't really a phony. Maybe he was just sick and tired of having to deal with those two.

I could relate.

And as to his hair?

Well, so what if it were a toupee?

Maybe it was best not have a shiny, bald head on TV.

Some people could do bald well. But maybe not him.

I looked at the man's cameraman.

"Were you on the chopper?" I asked him.

The man peeked from behind his camera. "Sure was," he said.

"Did you land first?" I asked him.

He looked upset.

"No," he shook his head. "We landed second," he admitted.

The guy was honest. I liked that.

So did Annie.

And apparently, so did Abbie.

"Close enough for me," Abbie said.

"Me, too," Annie added.

"*You* will get our exclusive interview," I finished.

The cameraman smiled widely.

So did the news guy. And *this* smile? Wasn't fake.

"So why were you home during a school day?" the man asked us.

We all rolled our eyes.

"Well, you see," Annie said. "It all started at school."

"She had to dissect a frog," I added.

"A live one," Abbie noted.

"After she killed it," I explained.

"But I *couldn't* kill it," Annie wailed.

"And she wanted to set the frogs free," Abbie added.

"So she started chanting," I told the man.

"Free the frogs," Abbie chanted.

"Free the frogs," I chanted.

"Free the frogs," Annie joined in.

"I could hear it down the hallway," Abbie explained.

"Me, too," I added.

"I knew Annie was upset," Abbie said.

"I *was* upset," Annie confirmed.

"I could feel it in my bones," Abbie mentioned.

"Triplets are like that," Annie explained.

"So I went to support her," Abbie said.

The man jumped in. "And you were going to support your triplet sister too?" he asked me.

He looked from the camera to me. Then back to the camera.

His smile was *huge*.

He seemed as if he were very happy that he'd just uncovered some great secret.

His smile was genuine.

"No. I was just out on a bathroom pass." I said. "I heard the commotion and was just curious."

The smile turned plastic again.

I felt sorry for the guy. I didn't *mean* to burst his little bubble there.

But then my mom came rushing through the door.

Guess her shift was finally over.

Great!

I'm going to get yelled at on live TV.

In front of all my friends.

Just great.

Maybe my mom wouldn't notice us.

But she made a beeline right for us.

"Are you all okay?" she asked us.

She gathered all three of us in her arms and squooshed us together.

"We're fine, Mom," we said in unison.

Abbie was pushing my face away from hers.

She almost stuck me in the *eye*!

"Are you sure?" she asked us.

"Yeah," I said. "If Abbie would keep her *finger* out of my *eye*!"

My mom reached out to me and started running her hands over me.

I knew from past experience that she was just checking for broken bones.

But to the TV viewer? It looked like she was feeling me up.

Great.

Just great.

How was I going to live *this* down?!

But before my mom could get her hands on anything too embarrassing, Dad came back.

Thank God for Dad.

"Oh, honey," she cried as she pulled him toward her.

My dad held his arms wide.

Encircling all of us kids and my mom.

Great.

We were having a Leeg-family group hug.

On live TV.

For all my friends to see.

Just great!

"I'm sorry I was mad at you," Mom blubbered to Dad. "About taking the kids on a high-speed chase."

"I'm sorry I had to take them," Dad blubbered to Mom. "But I couldn't let the robbers take Mrs. Farnsworth."

"I'm just glad that everyone is okay," Mom blubbered back.

Then she started slobbering big, wet kisses on all of us.

On live TV.

Great.

"Where's Mrs. Farnsworth?!" the bank manager said as he rushed into the precinct.

"I'm right here, Mr. Robbins," she called to him.

He rushed to her side. "Are you okay? We were all worried sick about you!"

She nodded. "Thank goodness for Jules and the triplets! The robbers were going to *kill* me! But the Leegs were right there, so I'm still alive!"

The precinct echoed with applause.

Mr. Robbins nodded happily. "Is this where I get my money back, Officer Leeg?"

"Sure is, Ned," my dad told him.

And then my dad hefted a huge duffle bag off his shoulder.

And handed it to the bank manager.

"This is fantastic, Jules!" Mr. Robbins said to my dad. "I mean, Officer Leeg."

"Don't thank me, Ned. Thank my kids," Dad said. "They split up and chased after the guys."

"Well then. I'd have to say they deserve a reward. Wouldn't you?" Mr. Robbins asked aloud.

Whoops and cheers were heard all around.

Mr. Robbins grabbed into the duffel bag and took out a fistful of money.

I had no idea how much was in his hand. But the bills were all hundreds.

And there was a *fistful* of 'em.

And Mr. Robbins? He had a *big* fist!

He handed the money to Annie, Abbie and me.

The news guy was smiling happily again. "So what are you going to do with all your money?" he asked us.

I looked at my sisters.

Annie shrugged.

For a split second I remembered the talk we'd had in the car with my dad.

"It's not enough to buy up all the schools. And then shut them down," I mentioned.

"Or start my own fashion line," Abbie added.

"Or buy a football team," I cited.

"Or a mountain," Abbie noted.

I looked at Abbie.

She nodded.

"So we're going to give it to our sister Annie," I said.

"So she can buy a computer simulation program with it," Abbie finished.

"A simulation program?" the news guy asked.

Everyone quieted down.

It was really weird.

I got a little embarrassed.

The cameraman peeked from behind his camera.

"You mean like a flight simulation program?" he asked. "Those are cool."

"No," I said.

"A golf simulation program?" Ned Robbins asked. "I have one of those."

He gripped an imaginary golf club. Then swung his arms.

"No," I said.

"A football program?" Officer Mahoney asked.

"No."

"A cooking program?" Gert asked.

"No."

"A drawing program?" the precinct sketch artist asked.

"No."

I hadn't realized there were so many different kinds of simulation programs out there!

"Well, what *kind* of program?" everybody chorused.

Annie looked at me.

I winked at her.

Her eyes sparkled.

"Really?" she said.

I nodded.